LILY'S London TOUR

A Travel Troupe Adventure

By Bailey Clark • Illustrated by Oksana Lysak

THE Travel Troupe

"Lily's London Tour" is a part of the book series "The Travel Troupe."

Explore additional titles in this series by visiting our official website at: TravelTroupeBooks.com.

Lily's London Tour: A Travel Troupe Adventure

Written by: Bailey Clark
Illustrated by: Oksana Lysak

ISBN: 979-8-9892929-1-2

For inquiries, please contact:
Bailey Clark
baileyclarkauthor@gmail.com
traveltroupebooks.com

To Mom and Chris,
thank you for believing
in me. I love you both!

Lily visits London, England's largest city.
She's heard of all the landmarks, each famous and quite pretty.
What better way to dash around than on the Underground,
She arrives at **St. Pancras Station**, with wonders all around.

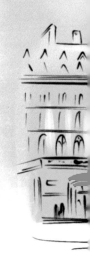

She's in the center of it all, as she makes her way through town.
Her first stop is **Trafalgar Square**, where she has a look around.

The National Gallery is on one side; to the other is The Mall,
The square is full of tourists; too many to count them all.

In the distance, down the Mall,
She spots a grand façade.
The sight of **Buckingham Palace**
Leaves dear Lily awed.
The scene is like a movie,
From the tulips to the guards,
It's a royal park-like setting,
With a majestic courtyard.

It's time for Lily to see some more,
So she heads toward the river.
In no time, she spies **Big Ben**,
If only just a sliver.
As she nears the clock tower,
She beholds the Parliament,
The **Palace of Westminster**
Houses England's government.

For a greater view of London, it's time to take a ride.
Lily climbs into the Ferris wheel known as the **London Eye**.
Gazing down from up above is a truly awesome sight!
She sees old buildings mixed with new, all from a great, great height.

From the Eye, she finds the **Shard**, London's tallest structure.
She heads toward the spire of glass to admire its architecture.

Ship masts and church steeples inspired this design,
A dramatic, new addition to London's skyline.

Near the Shard, there's lots to see just across the Thames (that's "temz").
She crosses over **Tower Bridge**, another of London's gems.
This bridge is more than pretty; it has a special task:
To open up its drawbridge when boats need to pass.

Up next, perhaps the best sight yet,
The **Cathedral of St. Paul**.
Lily can't believe her eyes,
That a dome could be so tall!
The magnificent design
Is considered English Baroque,
Designed three hundred years ago
By an architect's master stroke.

Lily's day has been quite busy; she needs a little rest.
So, she stops in for a spot of tea; in England, it's the best!
The **Savoy Hotel** is just the place for her little break,
She sips her tea, eats a scone, and has a mini cake.

Her next stop is a long way off, so Lily hails a ride.
In a black cab, she explores; every turn wide-eyed.

After tea, it's time to shop at **Harrods** department store.
The place is posh and polished, with merchandise galore.
She browses through the fashion halls, amazed by all the wares,
Then stops at Tiffany's Café to sample the eclairs.

It's time to take in British arts, and there is no better place
Than the **Victoria and Albert**, London's great showcase.
From Arts and Crafts to Rococo, Modernism to Nouveau,
The V&A has it all; the treasures overflow.

One last stop on this whirlwind day: a place for relaxation.
A walk in **Kensington Gardens** is her final destination.
Lily walks among the fountains, amazed by all she's seen,
London's history, art, and culture, and everything in between.

This adventure has been grand, amazing and swell,
But now Lily must bid you a fond and warm "farewell."

London

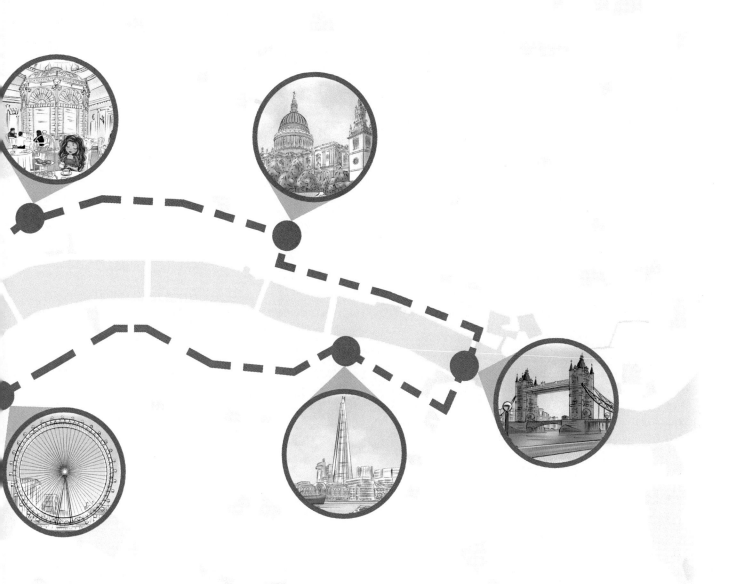

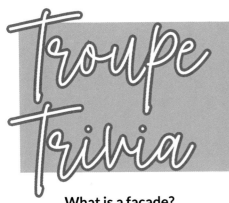

Troupe Trivia

Does your little explorer have questions? That's fantastic! At Travel Troupe, we believe that asking questions is the key to unlocking a world of knowledge. Our books were created to spark your child's curiosity, and here, we've answered a few questions that young explorers like yours might have asked while reading.

What is a façade?

It's the part of the building that faces the street. People design facades with beautiful decorations and materials, like stone, brick and paint. Some famous buildings have very detailed facades. So, when you see a building with a lovely front, you're actually looking at its facade!

What is the Underground?

The Underground is a train system in London. It's called the "Tube" because the tunnels it goes through are round, like a tube! It's a quick and easy way to travel. Riding on the Underground can take you anywhere you wish to go in London. It's like an adventure on its own!

Why is it called the London Eye?

The London Eye is a giant Ferris wheel, but it's not like one at a carnival; you ride in a bubble made of glass, so you can see all of London's amazing sights. It's called the 'London Eye' because it's like a huge eye in the sky, where you can see for miles and miles!

What's special about Harrods?

Harrods is a special store in London, and here's why: it's like a giant treasure chest! At Harrods, they have everything, from toys to fancy dresses to delicious chocolates. Harrods even has an Egyptian Escalator and an enchanted forest in the toy department.

What does English Baroque mean?

English Baroque is a style of architecture that was popular in England during the late 1600s and early 1700s. It's known for having symmetry, grand designs and decorative details. The buildings in this style often aim to create a sense of awe and amazement.

Why is tea so popular in England?

Tea is popular in England because it's a warm, cozy drink that most people enjoy. The English love it so much that they have a special afternoon tea time! It's often served with milk and sometimes with biscuits (cookies). It's a way for people to relax and socialize.

What do you do at Trafalgar Square?

There are lots of things to do while you're there: you can play, have a picnic, watch street performers, or enjoy the scenery. There's a big open space with fountains and statues. It is one of the most central spots in London, so it's an easy place to visit!

Why do boats need to pass through the Tower Bridge?

The River Thames (which is the river under the bridge) is like a busy water road for boats, and some of them are really tall. When a tall boat comes by, the bridge opens up so that a boat can safely move down the river.

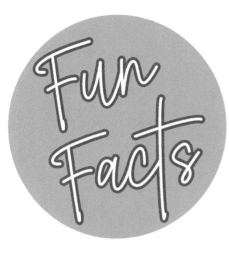

Fun Facts

St. Pancras Station has a super fast train called the Eurostar that can take you in an underwater tunnel, all the way to France and Belgium! Isn't that cool?

The Victoria and Albert Museum has a special room just for kids! You can see old-fashioned toys and even act like you're a kid from the past and play with some yourself!

Big Ben is not really the name of the clock or the tower; it's the nickname for the Great Bell inside the clock. This huge bell weighs as much as a small elephant!

Kensington Gardens has a pirate ship playground. You can pretend to be a pirate or explore like you're sailing the high seas. You can have your own adventure in the middle of London!

At 1,016 feet, the Shard is the tallest building in Western Europe. Imagine it's as tall as 87 giraffes stacked on top of one another – that's how high it reaches!

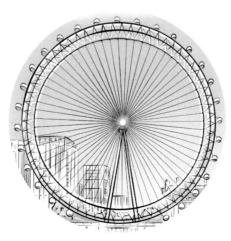

St. Paul's has a spot inside the dome called a Whispering Gallery. When you stand on one side, you can whisper something, and a person standing on the other side can hear what you said!

Made in the USA
Monee, IL
05 May 2024

58005737R00019